For our new baby,
Sylvie Anne

—H.M.E.

For Barbara Sobol with love

—L.R.

DR. DUCK
and the New Babies

by H. M. Ehrlich

with pictures by
Laura Rader

BLUE APPLE BOOKS

Text copyright © 2005 by H. M. Ehrlich
Illustrations copyright © 2005 by Laura Rader
All rights reserved
CIP Data is available.
Published in the United States 2005 by
🍎 Blue Apple Books
515 Valley Street, Maplewood, N.J. 07040
www.blueapplebooks.com
Distributed in the U.S. by Chronicle Books

First Edition
Printed in China
ISBN: 1-59354-073-6

1 3 5 7 9 10 8 6 4 2

Doctor Duck worked hard.
He was a busy man.
He saw a lot of patients
in his big red van.

Doctor Duck liked Sundays.
He gardened in the spring.
And when he took the day off,
he hoped no one would ring.

Doctor Duck was thinking
his planting should not wait.
Then three sheep came running
up to his garden gate.

The big black sheep was yelling,
    "Doctor, something's wrong.
A goat is having babies
    and it's taking much too long!"

Mother goat was bleating.
A baby goat was stuck.
She could not push it out herself.
But here comes Doctor Duck!

"Water, please," said Doctor Duck.
"Hurry up and run.
In just a few more minutes
this birthing will be done."

One baby goat was born,
then came Baby Two.
Doctor Duck was washing up,
thinking he was through.

"My, oh my!" said Doctor Duck.
"What is this I see?
Two little hoofs, a warm pink nose.
It's Baby Number Three!"

He tickled newborn noses,
    but he didn't mean to tease.
Baby goats breathe better
    after a good sneeze.

AH-CHOO!!

The kids were still quite wobbly,
though in a rush to suck.
Mother goat was happy.
"Thank you, Doctor Duck."

Doctor Duck packed his bag
and headed toward his van.
But someone else was calling;
it was the old bull, Dan.

"Doctor, please come look
    at dear, sweet Sarah Cow.
She's in the lower pasture
    and she's giving birth right now."

When the doctor got there
he gave a hearty laugh.

Sarah had delivered
a healthy, little calf!

As he passed the henhouse,
   Doc wondered what could be.
The hens were all excited.
   "I hope they don't need me!"

The hens called, "Doctor Duck,
go home and take a rest."
The biggest said, "I've laid 3 eggs.
They're safe inside my nest."

Doctor Duck got into his van,
all ready to go home.
He wanted no interruptions
from patients, friends, or phone.

Doctor Duck was planting,
although the day was late.
Then he heard a big commotion
outside his garden gate.

Two large pigs were yelling,
"Doctor, something's wrong.
A sow is having babies and
it's taking much too long!"

Thank you,
Doctor Duck!